THE FLOWER
OF DEATH

R.O.Clark

For everyone with Down's Syndrome...

FOREWORD

The Flower Of Death is a short story that will surprise and disturb the reader, and will show that nothing is ever as it seems...

Richard Clark has Down Syndrome and has written several books. He is a trustee of Saffron Walden Mencap and has a black belt in Karate. He especially enjoys writing science fiction and fantasy.

Gordon the Demon was walking home after he "stole" a book from the library. He did not steal the book, but the librarian accused him of it as he did not want him to take his books because "He will probably curse them!"

Some guards heard "he stole" a book and tried to track him down.

As soon as they found him, **Gordon** turned around to talk to them but when he did they ran off in fear.

After that **Gordon** went home to read the book, he got from the library earlier.

He was twenty-pages in when the book started to describe a flower that makes people like you.

Nobody liked **Gordon**...

Because he was a Demon everyone thought he would be evil.

He wasn't really and he wanted people to like him,

so he was very interested in the flower, and read all about it.

The author of the book said it was very hard to find this type of flower as they were extremely rare; only about four adventurers in the world had ever even found the flower.

They found them in the darkest forests, on the furthest seashores or on the highest mountains, anywhere far-away from civilization. `

"I am going to search for this flower. Even though I might have to search the entire world, I will find it."

Gordon said confidently to himself.

He packed and went to find the flower with his best-friend, which was his pet **Hydra**, known locally as Deathly, but only people from the village called him that. **Gordon** just called him **Hydra**.

Hydra was a beautiful male dark black and red hybrid Dragon.

Gordon met him and they left the village.

After walking for a long time they reached a deep dark forest. They searched there but couldn't find the flower.

Then they went to the seashore, where the ocean is, but still no flower.

Gordon climbed on **Hydra's** back and they flew over the ocean, hoping that perhaps they could find an island where the flower grew.

Eventually they came across an island.

Gordon gasped.

"**Hydra**" he said "Let's go down to that island, the flower could be right there in the mountains!"

Hydra roared to **Gordon** and he knew that meant 'Okay' So he just nodded back.

They hovered over the mountain and saw a black rose beneath them, and landed right beside it.

Gordon went closer, this was not the flower he was looking for, but he was curious as to what it was.

They looked into his book and tried to find if it was mentioned.

On page136 he found the 'Black Rose'.

The book said `Black roses are rare, there is a 0.001 percent chance that you will ever find one in the wild.

These magnificent flowers have a dark meaning, they can mean Hatred, Death, and Despair, however they can also give the owner of the flower great power.'

Gordon stopped reading after that.

He thought that If he could rule the village, and make good choices everyone would like him. He could even make some really good friends.

He stared out over the ocean and wondered if he should take the rose and keep it a secret.

He took a while, which did not bother **Hydra** at all. He just lay and slept on the ground. He was resting to regain his energy so that he could fly all the way back home.

After half an hour **Gordon** decided to take the Black Rose to his village but didn't think people would think it was such a great idea.

He turned to **Hydra** and said "We are going to take the **Rose**. We'll be leaving soon so make sure you are ready. We want to stay in the shadows, as we do not want anyone to know we were here except my parents. We may have one problem though..."

He pointed to **Hydra**'s huge footprints.

"Maybe it's okay. We can pretend those footprints were made by a wild Dragon."

He turned around and grabbed the flower although he kept the roots in the ground so that the Rose could grow back again.

"**Hydra** let's go." **Gordon** told **Hydra** getting on him.

"Roar."

Hydra roared and sprinted off the mountain.

They flew all the way back.

Gordon read more about the flower while they flew past the seashore, past the dark forest, then back to the village.

Gordon hopped off **Hydra** and took him to his backyard.

Then he walked in through the back door and said,

"Mother, Father I have found something that will bring us power."

His parents, who weren't demons like **Gordon**, turned to him confused, their heads tilted, and their eyebrows high in surprise.

They were obviously thinking "What does he mean bring us power? What could he have possibly found that would bring us power?

Gordon not knowing whether to speak or not, finally asked.

"What's wrong?"

His Mother said,

"Is this the 'Black Rose', the rose that means Hatred, Death, and Despair?

"Yes. We can use this against the village to control it." Gordon told them "All we have to do is put half a petal of the rose in their drink, let it sit for a while then the drink will turn black. When they drink it, they will feel one of those three things- 'Hatred, Death, or Despair' then we can use that to control them." Gordon paused. "I don't know if it's a great idea though, that's why I came to you first." he explained after he saw the surprised look on the face of his parents.

He did not know if the look was a good look or a bad look.

You are brilliant!" His mother suddenly yelled.

We taught you well my boy!" His father yelled too laughing happily.

"Shall we do it then?" Gordon asked

"Of course! Tomorrow at 2:00 P.M. That is the busiest time at the fountain." His mother explained.

"Then we will be there!" His father laughed.

"How about you give us the **Rose?**" His mother asked. "Sure." **Gordon** said and gave the rose to her. "I will be in my room sleeping. <u>Do not</u> wake me or get me up until then." He bellowed. He was becoming tired and grumpy after his long journey.

Gordon went into his room but instead of sleeping he thought of the village and its people. He began to feel worried and guilty; perhaps it wasn't such a good idea after all, but his parents seemed rather too keen to do it...

After lying in bed worrying he decided he was going to stop his parents from starting this war and prevent them from forcing the villagers to drink the black water.

He had to get ready to fight his family for the village.

Gordon would be their hero this time.

He fell asleep.

The next thing he knew was that it was already 1:30 P.M. and he only had 30 minutes to stop his parents.

Suddenly he had a better idea,

"Why don't I stop them when they are fighting the villagers." he thought "So they see me stop them and they can start calling me '**Gordon** The Hero'! I will be known by everyone and will have lots of friends!'

At 2 oclock he went to the fountain and saw his

parents go to the edge of the water.

"Oh Hello fellow citizens!" His father said very loudly.

People started panicking and tried to leave the area but could not because **Gordon's** Parents had added an invisible barrier that stopped them from leaving.

"Silence!" His mother exclaimed.
Suddenly...no one was panicking anymore.
It was complete silence, everyone just turned to see
Gordon's Parents and many of them were shaking with fear.
"You WILL drink this black water we give you. There are NOT any EXCUSES!!!

"Stop!" **Gordon** said and walked in front of them.

"Do not drink it!"

"What are you doing?" His mother asked, shocked.

Everyone in the village gasped.

"I will not let you hurt this village or the people in it." **Gordon** explained.

Gordon! Are you under a curse?"

His mother asked.

"No."**Gordon** said firmly.

"**Gordon**, we understand if you feel pressure to be on the good side, we feel your pain. We see through the tears in your eyes, the anger, and the bitterness in your spirit... Come **Gordon**. Come closer. Embrace the darkness once again." His Father said to him.

"No, I do not want to join your side."**Gordon**

declared.

"**Gordon** these people do not like you, they call you a villain because you look so bad. They will now only like you because you saved them, not because of your kindness. You were loyal to them, you gave them your sweat, your tears, and your blood. They still did not like you. They only know Demons as bad people." **Gordon**'s mother explained to him.

She turned to the villagers.

"Isn't that, right?" She asked them.

No one responded, they were all too fearful.

"**Gordon** I looked around at the people from the village. As a child, you were afraid of the dark and the monsters on the outside. As a man now, you run away from the light, afraid to show the monsters within."

"**Gordon**, open the cage that holds your rage.

The demon inside you never aged and with your darkness you will engage." **Gordon's** Mother said poetically whilst having an expression of -`this is your last chance if not we will not hesitate to hurt you. `

Gordon sighed.

His parents were right. Darkness cannot be destroyed; it can only be channelled. Human's will never stop hating people that are different, they will never stop warring.

He pulled himself up to his full height,

"I have now become death. I am not stuck here with you, YOU'RE STUCK IN HERE WITH ME!!!"

Gordon yelled "WE WILL SHOW NO MERCY AGAINST THOSE WHO DARE TO DEFY OUR POWER!"

"Yeah!" His mother supported him, though not in as loud a voice.

"WE ARE NOT VILLAINS; WE ARE JUST DRIVEN BY OUR OWN INTERESTS!" **Gordon** yelled some more.

Gordon and his parents ended up winning of course, and they ruled the village.

They made everyone drink the black water and **Malcolm and Rosie** (his parents) from then on always had everyone at their service, even if it was at 3:30 in the morning... and only because they wanted a drink of water...

H**ydra** got all the food and toys he wanted.

Gordon got to learn everything about flowers and could read all the books from the library he wanted.

Gordon had done his best to help people and make friends with them, and only some agreed to be friends with him for. "Being so brave!" or "You tried to defend us; but I know it is hard to face your parents."

It was not a happy conclusion for the villagers, but it was for **Malcolm, Rosie**, **Gordon, and Hydra.**

The End

ACKNOWLEDGEMENT

Thank you to Karmel and everyone at Saffron Walden Mencap's Side By Side Club...

ABOUT THE AUTHOR

Richard Clark

Richard Clark has Down Syndrome and has written several books. He is a trustee of Saffron Walden Mencap and has a black belt in Karate. He especially enjoys writing science fiction and fantasy.

Printed in Great Britain
by Amazon

85533654R10016